Put Beginning Readers on the Right Track with
ALL ABOARD READING™

The All Aboard Reading series is especially for beginning readers. Written by noted authors and illustrated in full color, these are books that children really and truly *want* to read—books to excite their imagination, tickle their funny bone, expand their interests, and support their feelings. With four different reading levels, All Aboard Reading lets you choose which books are most appropriate for your children and their growing abilities.

Picture Readers—for Ages 3 to 6
Picture Readers have super-simple texts with many nouns appearing as rebus pictures. At the end of each book are 24 flash cards—on one side is the rebus picture; on the other side is the written-out word.

Level 1—for Preschool through First Grade Children
Level 1 books have very few lines per page, very large type, easy words, lots of repetition, and pictures with visual "cues" to help children figure out the words on the page.

Level 2—for First Grade to Third Grade Children
Level 2 books are printed in slightly smaller type than Level 1 books. The stories are more complex, but there is still lots of repetition in the text and many pictures. The sentences are quite simple and are broken up into short lines to make reading easier.

Level 3—for Second Grade through Third Grade Children
Level 3 books have considerably longer texts, use harder words and more complicated sentences.

All Aboard for happy reading!

Library of Congress Cataloging-in-Publishing Data

Dussling, Jennifer.
    The bunny slipper mystery / by Jennifer Dussling ; illustrated by Joe Ewers.
        p.   cm. — (All aboard reading)
    Summary: When he wakes up one morning, Fozzie cannot find his fuzzy slippers,
so he calls on his friend Kermit the Detective to help.
        [1. Lost and found possessions—Fiction. 2. Sleepwalking—Fiction. 3. Puppets—Fiction.]
I. Ewers, Joe, ill. II. Title. III. Series.
PZ7.D943Bu 1997
[E]—DC21   96-39177
                                                                                              CIP
                                                                                               AC

ISBN 0-448-41562-3 (pb)   A B C D E F G H I J

ISBN 0-448-41615-8 (GB)   A B C D E F G H I J

ALL
ABOARD
READING™
Level 2
Grades 1-3

ᴛʰᵉ Bunny Slipper Mystery

By Jennifer Dussling

Illustrated by Joe Ewers

Grosset & Dunlap • New York

Ring! went the alarm clock.

Fozzie jumped out of bed.

His feet hit the cold floor.

"Brrr!" Fozzie said.

"Where are my slippers?"

Fozzie looked beside the bed.

His slippers were not there.

"Oh dear," he cried.

"My fuzzy bunny slippers are missing!"

Fozzie ran to the phone.

"I will call Kermit," he said.

"He will know what to do!"

Kermit picked up the phone.

"Hi-ho, Kermit the Detective here."

"Kermit, come quick," Fozzie said.

"My fuzzy bunny slippers are missing!"

Kermit came right over.

He looked all around.

"Aha!" he said. "A clue!

The window is open.

And there are footprints outside.

I bet the thief made them."

Kermit and Fozzie hopped out the window.

They followed the footprints

up a hill . . .

and down a hill.

They went over a bridge . . .

and under a bridge . . .

and back <u>over</u> the bridge again.

"This thief is making me dizzy!"

Fozzie said.

Then the footprints went backwards.

So Kermit and Fozzie did, too.

14

They came to an apple tree.

Kermit stopped.

There was a nightcap stuck in the tree.

"Look, another clue!"

Kermit said.

"That is not a clue," said Fozzie.

"That is my nightcap!

I bet the thief took it, too."

Fozzie took the nightcap

and put it on his head.

"Oh, that thief is very bad,"

said Fozzie.

"When I find him, I will . . .

I will make him write

'I am sorry' <u>ten</u> times!"

Kermit and Fozzie followed
the footprints around a birdbath
and up to a bench.

A teddy bear was on the bench.

"Another clue!" Kermit said.

WET
PAINT

"That is not a clue!" Fozzie cried.

"That is my teddy!

The thief took my teddy, too.

And now it is a mess."

"What a bad, bad thief!

When I find him,

I will make him write

'I am sorry' a <u>hundred</u> times!"

Kermit and Fozzie followed

the footprints down a street . . .

and up to a house.

"That looks like <u>my</u> house!"

said Fozzie.

"It <u>is</u> your house,"

said Kermit.

"Oh, that thief is bad!"

said Fozzie.

"I bet he came back to take more stuff."

21

Kermit and Fozzie

tiptoed up to an open window.

They peeked in.

"Do you see the thief?" asked Fozzie.

"No," Kermit said.

"But I do see something else.

I see fuzzy bunny slippers

next to your bed!"

Kermit and Fozzie went inside.

Fozzie picked up his slippers.

"Where is that bad thief?" he asked.

"When I find him I will make him write
'I am sorry' a <u>thousand</u> times!"

25

Kermit and Fozzie looked under the bed.

No thief.

They looked in the closet.

No thief.

Then Kermit saw Fozzie's pj's.

"Aha!" Kermit said.

"I know who the thief is."

Kermit pointed at Fozzie.

"The thief is you!"

27

"Me?" Fozzie asked.

Kermit nodded.

He held up Fozzie's pj's.

"Your pj's have paint on them—

just like your teddy.

I think you went sleepwalking

last night in your slippers

with your teddy bear and your nightcap.

Then you came home

and left your slippers

on the <u>other</u> side of the bed!"

Fozzie gave Kermit a great big hug.

"Thank you for finding my slippers,

Kermit," Fozzie said.

"But there is one last thing

I need you to find. . . ."

"What now?" Kermit asked.

"A pencil," said Fozzie.

"I have a lot of writing to do!"